People Of The Water

People of the Water

A novella of the events leading to
the Bloody Island Massacre of 1850

Kathleen Scavone

People of the Water.

A novella of the events leading to

the Bloody Island Massacre of 1850

Second Edition of People Of The Water,
ISBN-13: 978-0-9673981-9-8

Cover Photo by Kathleen Scavone
Copyright 2021, 2014 by Kathleen Scavone
https://www.kathleenscavone.com/

Cover designed and interior reformatting by Leo Baquero
leo_baquero@hotmail.com - www.layoutadaptationdesign.com

Acknowledgments

I would like to express my sincere gratitude to archaeologist, Dr. John Parker, of Archaeological Research, Wolfcreek Archeology, Lucerne, CA. He was very generous with his resources, time and expertise. He has an extensive knowledge of history, especially Lake County history, and is a tireless advocate for all things Lake County.

Thank you, and lots of love to my wonderful husband, Tom for his never-ending support of my endeavors.

I appreciate and love my sons, Eric and Justin on so very many levels, not the least of which is setting up my computer research 'lab' and initially formatting my book.

Many thanks go to Leo Baquero for all of his tremendous help with this book's 2nd edition journey to publication.

This book in no way represents the definitive work on the events leading to the Bloody Island Massacre, and any misinterpretations of the experts remain my own.

Foreword

The "People of the Water" is a story of one culture's love of life and the world around them. Through words, Kathy Scavone paints a picture that time-travels the reader back to a Clear Lake Pomo village in the mid 1800's. Through her own experience living on the land, she is able to weave into her story the natural beauty, wildlife, geology, and ecology of California's North Coast Range mountains and valleys as they are experienced for the first time by her two young main characters. Her extensive background research allows her to present actual Native American cultural traditions, technologies, beliefs, and knowledge as they would have been learned and experienced by these young characters. The arrival of Europeans and their disrupting interaction with the Indigenous People is explored as seen from the perspective of the Native Culture.

Though some of the actual events and experiences in the story are fictionalized, this is done only to provide a narrative flow as seen from the viewpoint of the main characters. All of the events and experiences outlined in the story are based on actual knowledge of Clear

Lake Pomo culture as provided by tribal elders that were interviewed by ethnographers in the late 1800's and early 1900's.

This story is a "must read" for anyone wanting to understand Native California lifeways just before the European invasion and the disruption that followed.

Dr. John Parker

Second Edition Introduction

As an impossible year rife with struggles of the pandemic, social, political, and climate upheavals which threaten our precious planet segues into 2021, our lives feel as though they are being remade during a profound test. All of these events may serve as more than a wake-up call, providing us with a reminder that all of us on this planet– be they people, animals or microorganisms are all interlinked. Old ways which were previously discarded, such as traditional languages, foods and land management techniques which draw upon native plant propagation and control burns are coming back, albeit slowly, full circle. The old ways, long over due, are gaining back much-deserved respect through a more inclusive atmosphere that is bigger than ourselves. Parallel to the aforementioned, the California Department of Education is renewing its effort to support Indian tribes and others to meet the culturally related academic needs of American Indians through addressing the widespread lack of knowledge and understanding of Native American history and culturally important information which was once glossed over and/or romanticized in public schools. The midden of the past offers us a window through which we can intuit the world as it once was. By acknowledging those who came before us, we allow history and nature to become teachers once again.

Introduction

During the seven years since this book was first published, the importance of respectfully and thoughtfully acknowledging the past of a significant event in the history of the Native People, the Pomo Indians of Lake County, California has become more vital than ever.

This is a fictional account of the events leading up to the Bloody Island Massacre of 1850. Like many Indians in California, the Pomo Indians of the Clear Lake Basin in California were run off of their tribal, ancestral lands, forced to work the ranches or Missions, beaten and massacred.

Charles Stone and Andrew Kelsey purchased stock from Salvador Vallejo, and garnered permission to use his land for grazing. Kelsey and Stone mistreated Indians to the extreme– they starved, beat, and worked them to death. It was common knowledge in nearby settlements that Stone and Kelsey were cruel to the Indians. The Indians could no longer tolerate the hunger and the beatings, so they killed some cattle for food. This incident did not bode well with Stone and Kelsey. Many more atrocities ensued– one Indian was tied to a tree then beaten, some Indian homes were burned down, and others were marched to the gold fields where most perished due to exposure and starvation. Added to those heartrending incidents was the fact that Chief Augustine's wife was kidnapped and forced to live with the white men. So, in the fall of 1849, Stone and Kelsey were murdered by Indians.

In the spring of 1850, a detachment of the United States troops led by Captain Nathaniel Lyon was sent from the San Francisco Presidio or Benicia with whaleboats hauled by wagons, along with cannons, in retaliation for Stone and Kelsey's deaths. Pomo people in their village of Badonnapoti on what is now called Bloody Island, on Clear Lake, California were targeted and massacred by the soldiers. Women and children were killed indiscriminately– soldiers chased them into the water, bludgeoning and shooting them. This massacre was replayed again and again over the course of a month as the soldiers continued killing Indians, working their havoc westward toward Ukiah. The United States government concluded its tyranny in 1851 by drafting a treaty and trying to initiate a rancheria. The treaty, like so many others, was never ratified. The site is marked by California State Historical marker number 427, located at the intersection of State Highway 20 and Reclamation Road, 1.7 miles southeast of Upper Lake. This marks the area, once an island, where this story took place.

California Indians have popularly been viewed as hold-outs from the Stone Age, "primitive", "savage", "lazy" and "stupid". Many people don't realize that California Indians practiced a subsistence economy and were a hunter-gatherer society. This was a well organized and systematic way of life which required an intense environmental knowledge. Acorns from many species of oaks provided a food staple, which was easily stored. The abundance of fish and game, along with the harvest of literally thousands of plant varieties produced food stores that surpassed what many North American Indians were able to procure through farming practices. Most California Indians had a "Chiefdom" society, private land ownership, stable political centers and territorial boundaries, far reaching trade networks, a money economy, resource and manufacturing professionals.

The brutality of the Bloody Island Massacre and similar atrocities to other tribes is a grievous legacy. The courage of the Pomo people lives on forever.

The Earth Sadly Wept

The Earth sadly wept
For the intruders who came in vast numbers
For the catastrophic destruction of nature
The uprooting of trees and families

Earth mourned the loss of forests for pastures
Star-thistles for grasses
Marshland for homes
Mining silver and gold clogged the streams

The world is remade-
It still speaks if we only listen.

Chapter 1

Springtime for the People of the Water was a time of celebration and giving of thanks. With the cold, wet winter behind them the people had much to be thankful for. Sweet clover carpeted the valley and provided a much-needed respite from the dwindling stores of dried foods. Clover's fresh taste was a delight to the taste buds. The vibrant green carpet was a welcome visual treat to catch sight of. It was a pleasure to leave behind the bleak monotones of winter's shrubs and trees and behold the unfurling of a bright new season.

The fertile valley where the People of the Water reside lies between two mountain ranges: the Mayacamas Mountains on the west, and the Bartlett Mountains on the east. Pomo is the name given to the People of the Water, who live near the Lake known as Clear Lake. Some say the word came from "Poma", a village, but in actuality it was a name given to the people by anthropologists at the turn of the 19th century. The basin's predominant feature, Clear Lake is magnificent. It is a lake that has maintained its vast shoreline for thousands of years, it being the oldest lake in the Americas.

The valley is dotted with oaks set like emeralds in a random pattern, with Blue Oaks and Valley Oaks predominating. It was the gentle, old appendages of a massive Valley Oak, gracefully cascading to earth and swaying in the wind, that once beckoned the villagers forth to rest and take refuge, as it is here that Djaska, a young boy, and his village-members live.

Djaska climbed the gently sloping hill above the village. Each damp step he took gave beneath him, but as he was small, his path did not leave deep imprints. The homes of the Pomo village looked like great sleeping turtles from up here! The homes, or tule huts were elliptical in shape, and about seven feet high. They had been constructed with pole frames and covered with a thatch of tule, a tall, prolific reed from the banks of the lake. The tule had been formed into bundles, then twined to the frame of each structure. A smoke-hole was crafted at the dome. Tule was also used to line the walls, for beds, and floor mats as well. Beyond the village he could see a large expanse of water– the lake which was so important to the villages that dotted the valley.

Mitabao, who was Djaska's younger cousin, showed him the place where the white men were said to have been seen. Elder Uncle, whose name was Antu, had told the story over the campfire. His stories were something the villagers always looked forward to. Uncle made his voice match the "chikago" of the quail or the howling of the wind. His stories were lively and animated to make a point, but this was a somber tale– one in which Mitabao and Djaska, even as children, could sense a foreboding.

Uncle's story of two pale men, each carrying game, wearing buckskin clothing and having faces full of hair, was told in a gray, glum tone. The message was clear– a big change was going to come over the lands of their people. The world will be much different than we have ever known it to be. There will be "talking lines," and strange animals with hooves and horns will one day encroach on our sacred hunting grounds. The elders then fasted and prayed for answers to the dilemmas presented in their visions.

Djaska could almost see those white men passing through the outskirts of their village. A shiver of fore-boding ran up Djaska's spine, but was soon displaced, as the village stirred with the new morning.

The sleeping hut of Djaska was the first to show signs of morning activity. Last night's cooking fire was brought alive by his mother, who disturbed the lazy coals with her fire stick and added pine and oak twigs to the now-hungry embers. Soon the flames were lick-ing their surroundings like hungry yellow tongues. She added cooking stones to the fire and took out a tightly woven basket which held acorn soup. The cook-ing stones were drawn from the flames with a special wooden utensil and added to the basket of soup.

Her families' acorns were stored in a cache built of tule. It had been carefully constructed with eight posts secured into the ground. The posts rose about six feet in height, with its floor being two feet off the ground. To this, an intricate framework had been built, similar to a bird nest, which could withstand the harsh winds and rains of winter.

His mother's skirt made a shushing sound against the woven floor mat as she quickly stirred the liquid, deftly assuring that the stones not be allowed to rest against the basket for any length of time, thereby scorching it.

The sweet aroma of the morning meal commingled with the smoke of the cooking fire, drawing Djaska down from his lookout. He ate hastily, as he was looking forward to taking out the fish nets and baskets to fish in the lake with elder uncle this morning.

Before fishing could commence, the fishermen purified the fishing nets and poles. "Why is it that you fill the basket with water and herbs, uncle?" asked Djaska.

His uncle had taken the special herbs from a pouch he kept in the sleeping hut and placed them in the water that was heated by hot rocks, in the same way that Djaska's mother had used hot rocks for cooking mush. "It is done this way for good reason," said Uncle. "Purifying the implements used to catch our food brings luck. Have we not always had plenty to eat?"

The carefully crafted fishing nets were then dipped into the fragrant concoction four times, then the poles were rinsed with the herbal liquid.

Each day the village took on a rhythm all its own. Every member knew what was expected of them. While the men of the village were fishing, the women were busy gathering herbs and roots. Some of the men had other jobs to do, like tanning deerskins, or making tools.

"Inform your father that we are taking our leave," instructed Elder Uncle. Djaska's father, known as Damot was also a fine fisherman.

The immense, sparkling surface of the lake reflected the billowing clouds that dotted the sky like so many dandelion puffs. A pair of courting Grebes called out across the lake– Kree! Kree! Their voices were shrill against the stillness of the morning. Djaska and Uncle watched as the black and white plumed aquatic birds rushed across the water, bodies nearly erect, their yellow feet stirring up the water's veneer.

"Uncle, tell me again of the story of our lake. How did it come to be?" Djaska spoke in a low voice. He knew to be quiet now as fishing time drew near.

Uncle patiently told the story Djaska wanted to hear. "Coyote caused a great world fire, then set about feasting upon all of the roasted lizards, snakes and other animals which were killed by the fire. This caused him to become very thirsty, so he set about to find some water. He went on a long journey across Snow Mountain. It was here where he met Bullfrog, who hid all of the water from him. In Big Valley, Bullfrog kept a large supply of water. Coyote drank and drank until the water was gone. Coyote felt sick from drinking so much water, so he lay sick for four days. Bullfrog began to doctor Coyote. Using an obsidian knife, he cut Coyote's distended belly open, releasing all the water. This water ran down and soon filled up the valley. Next, Coyote made all of the fish for the lake from the lizards and snakes he had gorged on earlier. That is how Coyote created Clear Lake."

While he was telling the story, Uncle placed the fish nets and poles in the tule reed boat, and they glided out to the favored fishing spot on the lake. The nets were constructed of milkweed fibers. Uncle and Djaska placed them in the water with care. A net was like a bag in the water. The mouth was held open by two cross-pieces of pine or fir. They were about ten feet wide and just as long. From this vantage point, the lake, with its 127 miles of shoreline, afforded a view of the lake's mighty sentinel, Mt. Konocti.

The morning passed with Elder Uncle telling more stories. Djaska listened and observed carefully, as one day, he too would be expected to pass the stories on to others. Theirs was a community of oral tradition; none of the rich tales were ever written down, but told and retold to keep the continuous flow of knowledge alive from generation to generation.

While dragonflies the color of blue jays swooped and circled about them nearby, the cacophony of the heron rookery in the trees lining the creek in the distance provided a familiar backdrop to the expanding day. It wasn't long before their fishing net was full.

The large expanse of water rippled and spat angry whitecaps in the wind of the late afternoon. The time for fishing was over, so Djaska and his uncle pulled their boat far into the reeds and up the shallow embankment, where it would sit until the next opportunity for good fishing arose. Other men and boys from the Pomo community followed suit, hauling in their fishing nets and heading to the fish camp not far from the lake.

The men of the village had been fishing these waters for as long as Djaska could remember. This was his 11th year. His father said that soon he would be taking the rites of the men which meant that he would be responsible for much of the materials needed for fishing– nets, traps and even a tule boat. He couldn't wait for his chance to join the fishermen in some night fishing sometime soon. Then, a fisherman needed to watch the time of night by observing the position of Big Dipper, or *baghal* in the sky. He would then know which fish were biting. But for now, he was still a boy, free to go along with his uncle for some of the day fishing and hunting expeditions.

Chapter 2

Summer was the season to journey to the coast. Father and Elder Uncle were taking Djaska and Mitabao on their first sojourn over the mountain, through the valleys, west to Bodega to the village of the Coast Miwok. Djaska had heard stories of the long and arduous walk to collect clamshells, mussels, to hunt sea otters, and collect food from the sea called sea lettuce. The stories had held him in fascination for years; there were narratives of bear encounters, of fording the swift, blue river, and sighting the largest of the ocean dwellers– a whale!

The Coast Miwok People had much in common with the People of the Water. They too, were hunter-gatherers who hunted deer, rabbit, and other small game, and also gathered acorns for a variety of uses. The men of the tribe wore a double apron-like loin cloth constructed of deerskin, with a tule or deerskin cape. Women wore fringed deerskin or tule dresses, or double aprons.

Plans for the journey to the sea were made well in advance. The men from the village readied their carrying baskets by packing much in the way of trade goods. They packed acorns, skins, fish, obsidian and magnesite beads. These unique, cylindrical beads were made from a special stone. Some were worn by the wealthy, and some beads were incorporated into decoration on baskets. They also brought striking strands of painstakingly crafted clamshell beads.

These beads were part of their monetary system, and an important commodity. Large strands of beads designated wealth in the community. The process of bead-making required much time, and was *not* an easy task. To the contrary, it was a specialized occupation. The shells were first collected, then broken into pieces. They were then smoothed into disc shapes by rubbing the shells on the rough surface of a stone. Next, a hole was drilled in the center of the bead. When the beads were strung, they could be smoothed into uniform and rounded shapes.

The profession of bead-making was inherited. The process was undertaken with utmost care. The bead-maker was sure to rise early in the morning to complete his task, having abstained from meat beforehand. It was important for the process of clamshell bead-making to take place outside the house. If this taboo were to be broken, then certainly the drill would break. The drill-bit was typically flaked from flint, while the string for the pump-drill was often made from sturdy woven grasses, or leather. In times past another type of drill was in use. It was a shaft which was rolled back and forth, by hand, on the bead maker's leg. When completed, the beads were carefully polished to a sheen on deerskin, each disc standing out like a full, white moon on a black, star-lit night.

Elder Uncle led the group of many villagers out of the valley they called home, early one morning. He had traveled the route to the sea many times and knew the trail very well. After they left the morning coolness of the lakeside, they began to ascend a scrubby, hot trail up, over the mountain. The terrain soon changed to that of lofty pine, oak, manzanita, and madrone with its smoothly muscular, man-like limbs. The scent of sweet, decayed wood– an earthy smell, permeated the forest floor. The forest devours itself in a continuous effort to start life anew. Mosses hung like shimmering green tears from the oaks. Above the oaks a turkey vulture swooped and glided. It had been hours since anyone had spoken, so intent were they on the quick, steady pace. The rhythm of the walk went on hour after hour, each man or boy bent slightly forward due to the weight of the burden basket, which was carried by a strap worn over the forehead, with the basket on the back.

With the evening beginning to close in around them, the group struck camp. Soon a fire was built, ready to accommodate their meal. Uncle started the fire with a

stick from the wild currant bush which he had packed
in his arrow quiver. Deftly, he twirled the currant bush
stick into the hole of another stick, with his hands.
Next, he added dried tree sap which had been pow-
dered, or some wood punk. When these caught the
sparks more kindling could be added. Sometimes, on
hunting trips uncle would carry the fire with him all
day. This was managed by carrying a glowing ember in
the bark from an oak tree.

Rabbits which had been hunted on the trail were added to a spit over the fire. If the rabbit had been hunted
at home, great care would have been taken to pre-
serve the rabbitskin, as a rabbitskin blanket was being made by Djaska's sisters. He pictured his sisters
back in the village with their glossy, black hair which
had been combed with a soaproot-fiber comb, and tied
back from their faces with cord made from milkweed.
Younger sister did not yet have her ears pierced. That
would happen when she had reached six or seven
years of age. Then, her mother would unceremoniously
pierce the lobes with a bone awl. The hole would then
be filled with maidenhair fern, adding more as time
passed until the hole was the appropriate size for an
ear plug. To sew a blanket, elder sister was taught to
be careful not to cut into the strip taken from the hind
legs of the rabbit. Then, using a nettle fiber string, she
placed it under the skin and sat across from her sis-

ter. They twisted the skin and the string into a large cord. It was left this way, fur side wrapped toward the string, to dry. Once the rabbit skins were dry a loom was built to weave the skins into a beautiful blanket. The loom was constructed with a series of small poles placed in the ground, with a sequence of cords running from each pole. The rabbit skin could then be drawn under and over creating the warp and weft of the blanket.

Soon the men and boys were content to be resting at last. The sound of coyotes yipping in the nearby hills accompanied the owl's hoots from the trees above.

Djaska whispered to Mitabao, "Owl is well-known for his talented nighttime singing."

"Yes," Mitabao added, recalling a story, "and Coyote wondered how Owl was able to sing like that. Owl told him that to sing like that he climbs up a tree into a hole to sing. But when Coyote tried doing that, the tree swallowed him and he died in there. Next, Woodpecker pecked a hole in the tree, found Coyote's bones and flung them to the Earth."

Djaska proudly finished the story, "It was Blue Jay who then came and squawked, waking Coyote from his sleep!"

The moon rose while the men talked of what the day ahead may hold. The boys drifted off to sleep, and dreamed of what they imagined the coast would look like.

Morning came quickly. Uncle was the first to awaken, then Djaska, and the rest followed. After a hasty meal of acorn cakes, they were back on the trail. Djaska could see the rest of his family in his mind. He was only a day away from home, but already he missed the fishing camp on the lake. He said, "It is good that Grandfather walked this trail with you many times. There is much to remember about the long walk to the sea!"

"Yes, it is true," said Father, "You must memorize many features about such a long journey. One day it will be up to you and your cousin to lead the way."

Djaska and Mitabao took care to pay particular attention to the trail after that remark. "The way is not difficult, but it is a long way. See how our grandfathers have worn a trail by taking this route season after season?" said Uncle.

The traders fell into the quiet, rhythmic walk of yesterday. Much of the terrain so far, had been familiar-looking. There were many manzanitas with their papery bark and small, red berries that made a refreshing tea. They passed through manzanita's older sisters, the madrone trees. They too, had bark which unfurled to reveal the silky, smooth trunk underneath. There were shade-giving pine trees, and stately oaks as well. The women of the village, if they had come along, would have busied themselves by collecting vital plants along the way, as they knew much about the various flowers, grasses, and roots, and how they are prepared into either food or medicine.

As they descended deeper into the valley, the vegetation began to transform. The trail became damp. The smell of the moist, live earth reminded them of home by the lake.

"If I were to dig a hole right here," said Uncle, "I would surely find fat earthworms and other moisture-seeking earth-dwellers in these rich, fertile grounds."

Here and there the trail was lined with grasses taller than the boys. Shreds of golden, dried grass clung to their damp skin. Soon the busy, bubbling sound of the river met them. It teamed with silvery fish slipping in and out of the shadows of the surging ribbon of water. Turtles with lustrous, earth-colored homes on their backs dove into the water with a 'plop,' their sun-baths temporarily interrupted by the group. Now, bay trees grew in profusion. These fragrant trees provided a respite from the hot afternoon sun. Their leaves swayed languorously in the breeze, softly whispering secrets to those who took refuge under their temporary shelter. They all loved the bay's pepperwood nuts, which could be roasted in a special way to be used sparingly as a condiment. Now there were alder, cottonwood, and willow trees. Thick stands of blackberries and grapes were found in abundance, their vines draping themselves and entwining any vegetation met in multitudinous embraces.

All at once the rhythm of their walk was interrupted, for out from the berry bushes across the river, a grizzly bear reared up on its hind legs, and pawing the air mightily, let out a ferocious roar! Her cub stood close by and curiously observed its protective mother.

Uncle said, "Stay perfectly still. Don't move." The group willingly complied. They stood stock still, barely breathing. Djaska and Mitabao's eyes were wide with fear. They had heard enough hunting stories to know that this encounter was dangerous. Even if they had been prepared with a large weapon, the bear wasn't hunted, as it was too much like a person. In their village there was, however a bear costume, worn by the bear doctor. This was stored in the woods like the deer costume, to be worn by a certain individual. When not in use, the costume was reverently stored in a hiding place with various pine seeds, magic herbs and charms which were placed in the costume head. If it was necessary to travel through bear country, herbs were useful for disguising the human odor. They were chewed as well as blown over the bear costume head. Next, the costume, or skin was swung about the head four times before it was worn. This costume was not in use for the trip to the coast, however.

The mother grizzly and her cub, sensing that the group across the river was somehow not a threat, returned to the shadowy depths of the brambles and resumed feasting on blackberries.

Father signaled the traders on, and they continued their journey– with a quickened pace for quite some time. Each said a silent prayer of thanks, as they felt very lucky, indeed, to have come to no harm by their encounter.

Father told of the white-skinned newcomers to the lands of coastal villages, and their disrespectful game of the grizzly bear. He said, "There are two, sometimes four men on horseback. As they ride toward the great grizzly, they seize its paw with a rope. They take turns tying up the bear and fastening the rope to the horn of their saddle, then, drag it to a tree. It loses its special magic. Sometimes they bring a bull and bear together to fight, only to watch them slaughter each other." Father shook his head sadly.

Before long, a rhythmic rumble-sound could be heard. Father, Uncle and the elders knew the sound, but it was brand new to the boys. "What makes that noise, Father?" asked Djaska. "It sounds like thunder!"

"That is not thunder, young son. Don't be afraid. That is the sound the ocean makes," father explained. "Thunder does not live far from here, though. He lives there." Father pointed to the north of where they stood. "Thunder lives in a house so clear that you can see through it. He lives with many kinds of fish, and when he says it is time, the door opens for the fish to run upstream to spawn. He possesses a great reflecting device so that he can see all that is going on in the world. The slightest move from Thunder causes the great thunder-sound. And when he holds aloft his great piece of crystal we can see bolts of lightening. We must not venture to the home of Thunder. It is dangerous to get too close to his home."

The footpath through the woods wound its way to open skies replete with immense clouds the color of great eagle's head. Suddenly Djaska cried out, "I can taste salt on my tongue, just as you described, Uncle!" The thundering sound of the ocean commingled with the sounds of crying, white gulls. At last they had reached their destination.

Chapter 3

The ocean was everything Uncle and the elders had described it to be– and more. It was so much larger than the boys could have imagined. It went on and on, to the ends of the world. It was as large as the sky, but a richer, deeper color of blue. In some places the land made a sharp drop to a rocky shore, and the sea beat against its walls time and again. Then, huge plumes of sea sprayed up to the sky like so many geysers going off. The earth here was comprised of silky sand the color of mother's favorite basket. Each time the waves left the shore tiny, blue-gray crabs dug into the cold, saturated sand. Birds that they later learned were called sandpipers, snatched up and devoured those who were not quick enough to escape. In the great rocks were pools full of unusual creatures. There were those shaped like stars the color of poppies, and others, also star-shaped that were colored like blackberries. Some creatures carried their homes with them when they walked. Djaska found a very pretty, uninhabited home and decided it would make a good present for his sister, Saiyai, whose name also meant 'something pretty'. In some places the rocks were lined with animals, circular in shape that displayed hundreds of feathery arms when the waters washed over them. When Mitabao and Djaska stood barefoot in the frothy ocean, it felt as though they were being dragged out by a great force. But the round-shaped animals that clung tenaciously to the rock stayed put. The boys saw a crab with a flame-colored shell plucked from the rocks by a gull. The wind blew cool and moist spray on their faces. It left traces of salt on their skin, and smelled wonderful and sharp– full of seaweed and fish. There was so much activity here that it was difficult to take it all in at once.

The water was many more times colder than the lake and stream waters of Mitabao and Djaska's experience. Djaska commented, " If I stand among these rocks for much longer, I fear that my reddened feet will be of no use to me, and I shall fall over!"

One of the local villagers who had been tossing pebbles into the sea, a boy of the same age as Djaska, said, "My uncle told this story when we had the last crescent moon: O' -ye or Coyote began to make people. He hunted for many kinds of sticks. He chose sticks that were hollow, like sage, and some hard sticks, like the oak and manzanita. He carefully set them aside, knowing that they would turn into people. Next, O' -ye placed the sticks all over the countryside– wherever he wanted people to be, that is where he placed them. Soon the sticks became the people. Where the sticks of hardwood were placed, these people were strong enough to withstand the cold, and where the sage sticks were left is where weak people live. They cannot stand the cold. My uncle said that since the white men came many people are dying. They must have come from Coyote's sage sticks."

As the boys explored the rocky shoreline, the coastal villagers prepared a welcoming feast. Great fire pits were prepared on the sandy beach. When the fires burned down enough, seaweed was cooked in ashes. Some seaweed was fashioned into cakes, like acorn bread. A variety of fish was prepared, along with abalone– the encrusted, oval shellfish that clung to the rocks. The insides of their shells were beautiful, rainbow-hued bowls. The villagers cut some of this meat into strips to dry in the sun. It could then be stored in baskets and kept for quite some time.

After much good food, the stories began to pour out of the men sitting around the fire. There would be plenty of time for trade tomorrow. Fog began to obscure the great water, sneaking in like a great grey wolf, but the sound of the sea was ever-present. Djaska and Mitabao found soft places in the sand to listen to the talk. Their faces gleamed in the firelight like sun-ripened acorns. Father and the other traders talked of the journey– the excitement of the grizzly bear encounter, how Djaska and Mitabao successfully completed their first trade journey to the coast.

Upon hearing about the trader's confrontation of a grizzly bear, one of the villagers began to speak of the bear's resemblance to people. "Bears look like great people." He made a wide, sweeping gesture with his hands. "They have hands like us, they stand upright like we do, and they are smart, like people. They can even understand what we say, and can hear us from a long way off. One day, long ago the bears of the woods nearby were seen dancing!"

The boys, who were getting sleepy, leaned in closer on their elbows and listened intently to the storyteller. "They were?" Mitabao asked incredulously. The boys didn't notice the smiles forming on the faces of the others.

The villager continued, "Os-soo'-ma-te, the mother grizzly bear even sang a song as she stood under a pine tree: 'moo'-oo, moo'-oo,' sang she. Her little cubs took hold of a pine tree bough and hung with arms above their heads and did a dance while swinging from the tree!"

At the conclusion of the story all of the men burst out laughing. One stood and pulled his neighbor up to join him in a clownish dance near the fire pit.

The sounds of the surf soon lulled the boys to sleep. It was then that the men began to speak of the terrible troubles that had befallen them of late. An intruder from far away was kidnapping members of their village and forcing them to work on land that had once belonged to them. This was happening with alarming frequency to other villages in the vicinity as well. Those who tried to come home were beaten. "Great long-horned beasts are grazing the lands once populated by deer and elk. Our women can no longer feel safe gathering the herbs and medicines needed in our village," said a villager, as he sadly shook his head.

The man of whom they spoke was Comandante Mariano Vallejo who was twenty-three years old when he was assigned to take over the position of the retiring Comandante Martinez. Originally, under Spanish law each mission was to be run by the Church for ten years, then, the lands were to be turned over to neophytes, as the Indians were called, as the Indian's property, while the missionaries moved to a new location to establish a new mission. Vallejo's responsibilities included leading the soldiers at the Presidio at Yerba Buena and the eight northern missions and pueblos. He had been awarded a 60,000 acre tract of land, the Petaluma Land Grant, by Mexico. The Indians were supposed to be paid from the mission's monies, from Spain. The money would also supply the missions with seed, livestock, and equipment to run the missions. The missions were thriving, from the standpoint of Vallejo and his men, providing the Presidio with woven wool blankets, leather shoes, candles, and food. The payments were to come from Mexico, but the money never arrived. Vallejo grew impatient with Mexico's promises, so he built up the Petaluma hacienda, then in 1836, a house in Sonoma. The building of ranch and home required a large workforce to complete. Indians were needed for such jobs as tanning hides, spinning and weaving wool, candle-making, farming and tending cattle.

Stories came to their conclusions and campfires died down. The illumination of the full moon was obscured in the night by a blanket of fog, which muffled the waves crashing on the rocks. The tide stole its way up the sandy shore like a stealthy hunter throughout the long night. It left tell-tale ribbons of seaweed all along the beach as proof of its having visited in the night.

Chapter 4

When the boys awoke to the ceaseless pounding of the surf, they were amazed all over again at the sheer size of the great water. They found that the tide left much more than tangles of seaweed. They saw an enormous, glistening grey fish beached on the shore. They ran to the trading camp. " Father, come quickly! See what the ocean has delivered to the villagers!"

Father, still sleepy, waved the boys away as though they were pesky flies and pulled his skin blanket up under his chin. "Leave me to rest. The night has not been a long one and we will have plenty to do once the others are awake."

Farther down the beach Uncle sat up curious about the commotion and, rubbing the sleep from his eyes inquired, "What is it, are you ill, young ones?"

"No, Uncle," said Djaska, "no one is ill. We have seen a fish that is the size of a small island! Look!" He pointed toward to the west.

Uncle looked out at the shore. "That's a whale! We must awaken the others before the grizzly bears get wind of it and come down to the shore to feed on it."

Others in the village had heard the sounds and awakened. The quiet village of the early-morning hours was replaced with a flurry of activity. They poured from their huts farther inland, and, at the direction of the headman, or Balaqui, of the village, began various tasks. The delivery of a whale to their shore was a great windfall. It would provide food for the whole village. Some began to get the fires going again in preparation for cooking, while others cut great pieces of meat with their sharp stone knives. Sea gulls swooped in for their share of the bounty, calling out in glee all the while. The sand was soon stained with the blood of the mountainous fish.

Djaska and Mitabao sat on the rocks nearby and watched, enthralled at all that resulted from the windfall. Djaska asked Uncle, who had been hauling meat to the fires, " Why did the whale leave its home to come to the village?"

Uncle replied, "The Balaqui of the village said it may have been sick, or driven here by other fish. No one is questioning it. They are just happy to have such a great food supply. Everyone will get an equal share."

Smells of smoke from the cookfires, and roasting fish commingled with the sharp salt air. Before long, all that was left of the whale was its imposing skeleton, which would be made into tools, ornaments, and many other items.

The next day everyone was ready to trade. "You watch carefully," Father said to the boys. "for one day it will be your turn to bargain with the village."

"Everyone is sure to leave today with something they must have," said Djaska. "They are sure to take a liking to our beautifully crafted arrowheads."

"And we know that we will take plentiful clamshells so that beads can be prepared," said Mitabao.

"You're both right," said Uncle with confidence, "we all look forward to this long day of trading."

Items of all description were carefully laid out by all who joined in the trade. Placed on mats on the beach were roots, seal skins, fishhooks of iridescent abalone, shiny black obsidian arrowheads, magnesite beads, dried kelp, surf fish, baskets, and many other trade goods. It was imperative to have a sharp eye for the best they had to offer.

Chapter 5

The journey home to Clear Lake was uneventful. Cooling coastal fog followed them until they reached the ridgetop. It seemed to Djaska and Mitabao that more effort was required for the trip home than the trip to the coast, but the traders were tired from the long nights of story-telling and the intensity of trading their goods. At last the waters of Clear Lake danced and gleamed before them like a beautiful abalone shell in the sunlight.

"Look!" announced Mitabao, "There is younger cousin in his tule boat."

The village homes shone like wet sand in the glow of the afternoon sun. It had been a very interesting journey, but the familiar sites of their village were most welcome! He dropped his carrying basket near the family's hut and, grinning happily greeted Grandfather. Before running down to the lake, Mitabao stated, "I have much to tell you, Grandfather!"

Djaska and the rest of the traders followed. "Grandfather! The ocean was even more splendid than your stories foretold! The waves were like angry giants thundering their mighty feet! There were black, shiny cormorants that flew out to the great rocks and stood like lookouts guarding their domain! And the whale! A great fish came to sleep on the shore; it was as large as Kam'Dot Island!"

Mitabao added, "The land of the coast is unusual! There are lagoons, bays, and tall, tall cliffs!" Grandfather, who was busy chewing sinew in preparation for bowstring, smiled in response to the boys' colorful descriptions.

The traders busied themselves with the routine of their own village life. Djaska reflected on the log rafts of the coastal village, and the striking difference to their own boats, which were constructed of tule reed. Their own boats were assembled from bundles of tule, and could accommodate three or more people. The front of the boat rose to a proud peak, and the sides diverted afternoon waves from entering the craft. Uncle and Djaska had assisted in gathering tules, tall, green reeds which grow around the lake. It was a versatile plant, useful for constructing boats, huts, mats for sitting upon, and other uses. The plants were cut about six inches from the ground with an obsidian knife. If cut any closer to ground-level, the plants could be damaged, die, or may not grow back for the next harvest. They had taken care not to reap the whole tract, but to take from different sections, again so as not to deplete their valuable resources.

Mitabao's baby sister was swaddled securely in her cradle near their mother. This unique baby basket served several purposes. It kept the baby safe from numerous potential hazards like scorpions, rattle-snakes, and poisonous plants. The cradle basket also produced a feeling of security, like that of the mother's womb. The baby was kept clean and dry with plenty of protective willow bark. The shredded bark was changed, washed, and used again before discarding.

His older sister was residing temporarily in the small, tule menstrual hut. Before its inhabitation a fire had been built in the hut, then the burned-down coals were spread over the fire-pit area, and finally, doused with a little water. Next, tule was laid across the coals, with a comfortable layer of shredded tule on top. This was repeated daily. Her diet at this time could not contain fish or meat. Instead, she consumed pinole and mush. She had undergone a special ceremony before entering the hut for the first time when she was given a panther robe dress, buckskin skirt, and a hairnet. After this she was given a basket of acorns and instructed in the preparation of acorn mush-making.

Mitabao was in his tenth year, and like all boys of the eight-to-ten-years age range he had come of age and would soon become a man. He would then partake in a special ceremonial bath of angelica root water. Prior to the ceremony he would don a special, beaded hairnet. A great feast would ensue, and he would be presented with gifts such as bows and arrows. He would be instructed in the sacred ways of hunting. The elders would speak their hopes for the boy. The importance of man's place in the world with animals and plants would be solemnly spoken of. In the world of the People of the Water it was vital that the natural world was not abused nor taken for granted, but, conversely, respected and reverently appreciated.

Chapter 6

The sun brought new growth and vibrant energy to the village and everything took on a more brilliant hue. Muddy paths gave way to lush, green corridors. Birdsong wafted along the gentle breezes and cold, wind, and rain were fading into distant memory. Now was the time to feast and dance! Time to invite the neighboring tribes to share the bounty.

The People of the Water marveled at the differences amongst these neighbors. Their language, customs, and stories were different from their own, but it was always good, in the end, to learn more of these strangers, to trade with them, to be entertained by them after a long winter.

Ah, the great delicacies they would consume then! There would be juice from the elderberry and manzanita berries to enjoy.

There may be Crane to dine on at the feast. Crane was caught with a hook and line. The hook was carefully constructed from a rabbit's leg bone. It was pointed at one end and notched in the center so the line could be attached. A small fish was used as bait and laid on the tules near the shore, then eaten by the crane and caught. Not only was the crane used as food, its leg bones were used for earrings, feathers for blankets and headbands. The bone was sometimes made into a whistle, while its bill helped shred tule.

The deer consumed at the feast would be hunted by those specially trained for the job. Hunters took great care throughout the hunt to follow the traditional procedures by chanting hunting songs both before and during the hunt. He fasted and prepared by rubbing himself with angelica and pepper tree leaves. He prayed. He built a strong fire before the hunt, creating smoke by burning more angelica and pepper tree leaves. In the same smoke, he held aloft, over the fire, the tools he needed: quivers, bows, arrows, and deer-head disguise. Dried meat from the deer could be kept for four or five months.

Bows of many kinds were used. A good hunter knew just which one to utilize for the hunt. A bow could be constructed of yew, nutmeg, or mahogany. This kind was custom-made by measuring from the center of the hunter's chest out to his fingertips. It was usually one and a quarter inches wide. A bow for big game hunting was larger than that of a duck-hunting bow and was decorated according to the hunter's wishes. Constructed from hard wood of an evergreen tree, its length was measured at twice the length from the hunter's fingertips to his elbow. It was one and three quarters inches in width, narrowing slightly at the handgrips. Another type of bow which was used was for small game such as squirrels and birds. Willow or dogwood was used for some small game bows, which were undecorated, and instead of sinew, a string constructed from nettle fiber was used. Arrows of many kinds were employed for hunting, depending on the type of game being sought.

Also employed for hunting was a type of catapult using a stick placed in the ground to heave stones at nearby small game. Rocks were slung at game through the use of a type of sling as well. This sling was made of sturdy deer hide in the center, or pouch, which was cut about two inches by four inches in length. Attached to the pouch were two and a half foot long fiber strings with a loop handle. To hunt using this method, clay balls or round stones were used. Those made of clay which had been fired were preferred because of their lighter weight and because they had the ability to kill three or four mud hens at once as they skimmed across the lake. To use the sling, the hunter placed the clay ball in the leather pouch and folded it over. Then he would place his middle finger into the string loop, bringing the other end of the string into which a knot had been tied, together in his hand. Around his head the sling would be spun, releasing the projectile to its intended target with a deft hand.

A good feast and dance would make certain that the harvest season in the fall was successful, and that there would be plenty of game, roots, acorns, and a myriad of other foods for everyone. For the feast to ensue, it would be necessary for a messenger to be dispatched with the invitation. The news would be announced to the neighbors with a message string. This string would have a knot tied in it for each day that remained before the spring festivities were to begin. The headman would know when to arrive by untying a knot each day, beginning with the day he was left with the string.

The days before the festivities were busy ones. The roundhouse was prepared by special members of their society. There were consultations with the Balaqui, or village captain, on which site to use for its construction, which trees could be taken, and to determine the exact placement of the sacred pole. There was much to do in the spring.

Chapter 7

Djaska called to his uncle, "Look at the earthen cloud that rises from below! What can it be?" He was breathless, having run back to the village, his eyes wide with fear at what he'd witnessed.

Uncle peered out in the direction indicated by Djaska, his face masking the alarm he, too felt at the site beyond.

"The earth trembled like the hills were going to topple, uncle!" Djaska issued excitedly. "I thought Konocti was coming alive again, like in your story." He was referring to the story of the sacred mountain of obsidian that stands like a guardian, nearly 4,000 feet high on the placid shores of the lake. The obsidian obtained from this area was vital for the myriad of tools and weapons fashioned from the glass-like stone. It was invaluable as a trading commodity as well, as it was traded up and down the land for great distances.

As the thundering sound increased, so did the dust cloud accompanying it. The other members of the village put down baskets which they had been weaving, stone tools they had been chipping and acorn meal they had been grinding and gathered to watch the spectacle below.

Besides the thundering, there could be heard great bellowing, deep resounding noises, along with the occasional higher pitched bleat.

Soon the great noisy dust cloud made its way along the creek not far from the village. The intensity increased– it could now be felt as well as seen and heard. The ground resonated, vibrated. The force was unstoppable, frightening the villagers.

It was now clear that the event they were witnessing wasn't a volcano or an earthquake. Large, brown hoofed animals with long, pointed horns were the source of the commotion. There were hundreds of them snorting, blustering, and charging down the creek, accompanied by a vaquero on horseback.

The Balaqui of the village said, " We have known of this day for some time. Grandfather foretold it. The villages of the coast have seen this. The white man's cattle runs free on our land now." He looked neither frightened or surprised, but instead, resolute. "Go now," he nodded to three villagers, "Watch from the knoll above and tell me in which direction they choose for their animals to inhabit."

An air of quietude overtook the village as they awaited the watchmen's report. The Balaqui called a council meeting. He had many responsibilities to his people. He took his job of overseeing his people very seriously. He ensured that even the poorest members were fed and clothed. He did this by accepting extra rations from others to give away. He looked after widows of the village, safeguarding them in their unfortunate circumstances. He used his power to settle arguments when needed. Among his gifts was the ability to give great speeches. Although his position as Balaqui held great prestige and he was looked up to; he was greatly respected by his people, he did not allow power to corrupt him. Being a fair and wise man, he knew that would be morally wrong. He also knew that he held little political power and understood that a proper society required a balanced, stable, yet subtle form of government.

Later, the watchmen returned with their news. The report was not a good one for the People. There had been hundreds of cattle driven into the valley by vaqueros, or men on horseback. Some of the watchmen knew the language of the intruders, having been taught by the coastal Indians. "They are brothers of General Mariano Vallejo, from the mission that lies below the mountains, in Sonoma. Their names are Juan and Salvador Vallejo."

The watchmen continued their surveillance over the course of a few weeks. The Vallejos camped in the area of the feast of last fall. Then, the grounds had been teeming with gambling games played with the neighboring village, laughter, and the sights and smells of cooking. Whenever there was an overabundance of food, a great feast would ensue for all to partake. Now, cattle trampled and ate down whatever was in their path. The havoc and destruction caused by these lumbering, unwieldy beasts must surely stop, but how and when?

Chapter 8

Uncle concentrated on the black and white bird in the hole in the tree made by that bird– a woodpecker. He deftly placed a basket over the opening to catch the noisy bird. The bird would not be eaten– that was forbidden, as woodpecker was the oldest bird in the forest, and thereby special. The chief would be pleased with the bird's quills for his belt. He called it "tsapa put ema`" or "looks good belt." Women of the village also desired the distinctive feathers for dance ceremonies and basketmaking.

Basketmaking required much training and preparation. The People of the Water were considered to be the most highly skilled of all villages in this occupation. Their fastidiously woven baskets were sought after and prized all over the land. The techniques they employed displayed their great variety. The coiling and twining of their baskets was intricate and diverse. Feathers of mallard, meadowlark, oriole, woodpecker, and other birds were incorporated into the design of some baskets.

As he carefully worked in the tree that gave his family its acorns in fall, he saw hummingbird whoosh by like a dart. Hummingbird was another special bird not to be eaten, as it was guarded by thunder god.

From his vantage point, aloft in the tree Uncle watched a gambling game occurring on the ground not far from where he was hunting woodpecker. The men played a game using pairs of two and a half inch long bones. One bone was differentiated from the other with string tied around it, while the other was left unadorned. Although two were playing, many more could play this exciting game. The players each held two bones and began by mixing them with a handful of grass behind their backs. The gambler's job was to guess which bone was held in his opponent's hand.

"Ah, you are very lucky!" called out one gambler to another.

"It is not luck that I possess, but skill!" laughed another.

Viewing this game brought to mind the variety of games at the spring feast. At past gatherings there were ball games using a ball made of deerhide, which was stuffed with shredded soaproot. Another game included sunflower leaves bunched together to be used for archery practice. Some played games with dice that were made from walnut shells that were filled with pine pitch and decorated with abalone shell.

The game of staves was a versatile and popular game, and like some of the other games, special songs were sung to ensure good luck. There are many ways to play staves. One way to play is to place ten counting sticks near the edge of the animal-skin blanket. The person designated as starter holds six staves in her hand and tosses them onto the center of the blanket. She can receive points if all six black, or patterned sides face up. Then the player takes three counting sticks from the edge of the blanket. If six white, or undecorated sides face up, the player takes two counting sticks from the edge of the blanket. If the staves land with three white and three black sides up, the player takes one counting stick. If any other combinations occur, no points are scored. Every time a point is scored, the player takes another turn, until his luck runs out. When all counting sticks have been taken, players then take sticks from their opponent. The game can continue for days until one player wins all ten counting sticks!

Other amusing games for girls and boys included one played with a tule fiber ball. First a circle was formed, next the children tried to keep the ball in the air. Uncle remembered that Djaska and Mitabao especially enjoyed tag, which could be played both on land and in the water. The younger children took pleasure in spinning acorn tops, spinning the small toys for hours.

Chapter 9

"Is everyone prepared for the burning of the ground?"
Father cried out.

"We're ready for the burn!" announced Elder Uncle.
That meant everyone needed to do his part to aid in the
controlled burn of the valley floor. The men controlled
the burning while the women watched the homes. If
fire began to encroach, it was extinguished by beating
it out. The People of the Lake were both hunter-gath-
ers and horticulturists due to their practice of utiliz-
ing their environment for maximum yield via control
burns. The grasses were winnowed for their seed, then,
after the grass seed was harvested, they dug holes at
intervals throughout the meadow, approximately one
and one-half feet deep. The field was then set afire. The
parched seed was then re-collected, then ground, and
finally cooked into a bread or mush. This control burn
served many purposes. It killed undesirable plants and
insects, enriched the soil with ash, and it protected
the village from wildfire. As an added bonus the mice
and shrew which had taken refuge in the strategically
located holes were collected, ground up, and savored
as a delicacy. Fire benefited the valley floor in many

ways. It increased seed production, stimulated growth
of ceremonial wild tobacco, protected the villagers
from snakes, and increased visibility. The ground under acorn oaks was burned every three years.

The sun-colored flames licked and consumed the
dry land, sending curls of dark, ghost-like smoke up
in the air. The practice was both exciting and hum-
bling, as it raced across the earth taking from it the
old, and at the same time providing a fertile new me-
dium for spring's regeneration. It was a stunning sight
to behold when at last the vivid new shoots sprang
from the seemingly barren earth after these burns.

A posse soon diverted the villager's attention. Several of the bearded newcomers galloped into view, obvi-
ously distressed. They whooped, hollered, and reared
up on hind legs of the mighty beasts on whose backs
they rode, alarming all in the vicinity. One yellow
haired man yelled, "What do you think you're doing?
You're going to set the whole valley on fire!" As he said
this, he began swinging a huge coil of white rope over
his head. He then threw it toward Elder Uncle Autu,
encircling him with the white snake-like loop, catch-
ing him in its hub. Other bearded men followed suit,
snaring others from the village in their loops of terror,
dragging them away.

Djaska screamed, "No! Father!" His father, Damot
was also dragged violently away.

Others yelled, "Stop! Stop!" They began to run after the helplessly snared victims, but to no avail. The horses the men were riding made swift work of the many kidnappings.

Chapter 10

This was a heartrending time, not only for the People of the Water, but also for villagers all up and down the great coast. The bearded men kidnapped fine, strong men– and women from all around the vicinity, even Yokia and Potter Valley. They were forced to work for ranchers called Charles Stone and Andrew Kelsey.

The ranchers were talking about an Indian scout from another village who showed a carpenter named James Marshall, from John A. Sutter's Fort, a good place to build a sawmill. Sutter wanted a sawmill built in the foothills in the Sierra Nevada Mountains so that more settlers could move in and build houses on the other villager's lands. The scout took Marshall up the American River to the village of Koloma, belonging to the Maidu people. Here, in the river the scout and Marshall found gold. Gold was bringing ranchers and their captured slaves to work in the cold river to mine the gold. They used mining tools like pans, rockers, and long toms. Villagers shoveled gravel from the river into one end of the rocker, then others were made to pour heavy buckets of water over the gravel. Riffles in the bottom of the rocker collected the gold for the ranchers.

Mining for gold was very hard work– especially since they received very little food. The pay, a pair of overalls and a bandana did nothing to assuage their hunger. Many villagers died of starvation in the gold fields and of exposure on the cold and unfamiliar routes to and from. The villagers did honest work, but were flogged anyway because Kelsey and Stone thought they were stealing gold.

Stone and Kelsey used the People of the Water as their own personal pack animals, heaping mining supplies on their backs to be sold to other miners. They left many of the People of the Water to fend for themselves, while they rode back to the ranch on horseback. Many Indians were shot in the Sierra Nevada Mountains, as then, the custom was to look upon Indians as bears, to be shot on sight. The language of Indians who lived in this area, such as the Maidu was foreign to the People of the Water, adding to the danger they faced in the long journey home. The journey was so hard, only one villager who was forced into the gold fields survived to tell the others of the atrocities of this mining trip.

It took a large workforce of kidnapped villagers to construct Stone and Kelsey's adobe homes at the ranch. Making all of the adobe bricks needed for these homes was exhausting work. Water from the stream was carried by baskets to mix into the clay, straw, and cow manure. It was necessary to slog around in a pit to mix the ingredients with bare feet. The adobe was placed in wood forms, which were also constructed by the villagers. When nearly dry, the forms were lifted for reuse, and the bricks were left to dry completely in the hot, summer sun.

All who labored in the scorching, summer sun felt grim and defeated. The motion of their daily routine seemed unending. With torsos bent they lifted the heavy adobe forms. Shoulders strained while perspiration formed rivulets down their backs.

Uncle retrieved heavy, dry adobe bricks until he felt numb. He met several others at the brick site, who were laboring equally hard. He couldn't hide his feelings about working like this– he looked disgusted. He felt their anger grow with his. They hated the bulky, brown bricks in front of them. They hated them for the homes they would ultimately create for the crazy bearded men. They hated the hard wood forms that shaped the unending, massive cubes of clay. Their whole world narrowed to slogging in a mud pit with the ultimate goal being to satisfy other's greed. Grief for those who died along the gold mining route further colored their days a bleak gray.

Throughout the day the only food rations they received was a little meat. This beef, as it was called had a foreign flavor. They were not permitted to hunt and gather food in their traditional ways any longer. Even if they had been allowed, the destructive grazing of the cattle had destroyed their hunting grounds. The birds, rabbits, deer, herbs, and roots they had subsisted on for thousands of years were no longer present. The villagers who had fled to hunt the once bountiful grounds were captured and beaten by the bearded ones. Once vital and robust, the People were now in a weakened state.

There were many tasks required of the villagers now. Some were sent to the fields where the once proud and prolific oaks used to stretch their luxuriant limbs. Now a vast grassland of oats replaced the trees used by generations of their people. Villagers were required to cut the oats with shiny, sharp tools the bearded ones called steel blades. It was hot, tiring work to bring the blade back and forth among the oats time and again. The grasses were placed onto piles, with the workers laboring to scoop up pile after pile, knot them together into bundles, thereby preventing them from lying on the damp earth and rotting.

"Why do the bearded ones cause us so much agony?" One of the villagers asked under his breath. If conversation were detected during their labors they would surely be punished. Punishment was meted out for no apparent reason; it could come out of nowhere.

"They are greedy beyond compare," another whispered angrily.

"Yes, they take, take, and take, but have you ever seen them offer thanks to the gods? The abundance that was once all around us was put here for many and all, not just for some." He thought of the many prayer songs and chants spoken by the village doctor. There were over one thousand. As he conversed, so did his complaining, hungry stomach.

As they spoke amongst themselves they could hear the familiar, rhythmic tapping of mortar and pestle. The village women were pounding, laboring to make flour for the ranchmen. In recent times, before they were forced to become slaves, they would harvest acorns when they were dry. Djaska climbed a tree and struck the acorns down with a stick. The villagers would carry their large, cone-shaped baskets on their backs with the use of a strap that stretched across their foreheads. About eight of these baskets would fulfill a family's acorn requirements for the year. After the acorn was hulled it was pounded into meal with mortar and pestle. Another of their many unique baskets would be used in the process of grinding. This one was bowl-shaped, but with no bottom to the structure. The basket became a hopper, which allowed more acorns to be ground at once. Leaching took place next, by the continuous pouring of water over the meal. This took place in a special sand pit which was prepared ahead of time. After several hours of infusing the meal with water the tannin, a toxin, was removed. Next, the meal was ready to make bread or soup. It was poignant to see women who should have been filling the village stores with traditional acorns, and instead were forced to sweat and toil for the ranch grinding flour, with small compensation. The Indians were starving now.

"Young one, please come here!" A villager called softly to a young village boy, who complied, running swift as a deer to find out what the elder villager wished. "Ask the wife of the rancher if we may have a bit of that wheat that is being ground. We are very hungry and need more than the ration of beef to keep working like this."

"Yes, I can do that," the young boy nodded, then walked up past the newly constructed fence which was built by the villagers to the specifications of the ranchers, Stone and Kelsey. The villagers watched as he met the wife at the door of the adobe home. She smiled at the boy, and then poured some of the precious grain into a burlap bag! The villagers salivated at the thought of the taste of some food. They could ferret some back to the elders who were as hungry, if not more so, than they!

Next, a picture of horror was played out before their eyes. One of the ranchers came out from behind the house, drew his weapon and fired upon the helpless boy. "Thief!" He yelled. As the boy's body went down, the sack of grain spilled in an arc all about him. The ranch chickens began to assemble and peck at the grain, oblivious to the terribleness of what had just occurred.

Chapter 11

It was a time of great mourning for the slain young one. The wailing of the villagers could be heard for a great distance. How could one so young be taken from them– and for no logical reason? This was indeed a time of great sadness. The boy's body was lovingly placed in the house of his parents. Respect was paid to him by many visitors. Mourners placed much-loved robes over him as they proceeded somberly by him. Many gave valuable beads and good baskets as parting gifts.

After the required four days, the boy's parents desired the funeral. The boy was lifted with his shroud of robes, beads, and baskets onto a stretcher with long poles with which to carry him to the cremation site, about a half-mile away.

"Tell your people to quit their catter-walling," directed Stone to the Headman. "I've had enough of that noise." With that abrupt admonition Stone yanked the reins of his glossy, white horse, spurred its sides, and rode off.

The dust that Stone's horse stirred up settled around the villagers like a dark, menacing cloud, adding to

the somber mood they all felt. Each of them had reason beyond the tragedy that had recently occurred for
hating the men who forced them to give up their way
of life, their land, and the ways of their ancestors.

Not everyone in the former village was allowed to pay
their respects and mourn their loss in a traditional,
dignified manner. Stone and Kelsey made it clear as
only they could, that it was business as usual on their
ranch.

It was required of Autu and Damot that they round
up wild cattle that had escaped the herd. In silence
they approached the corrals that were already full of
noisy, restless cattle. They mounted chestnut and bay
horses, leaving the cacophony of the corral behind
and headed into the woods and valley that had been
sacred to them. The rawhide reins, fastidiously braid-
ed by Autu and Damot were already well-worn, but
proved to be stronger than the single strap they were
originally made to use by Kelsey.

The once prolific grasslands were now sparse and
dusty. With each beat of a hoof a cloud of dust sprang
forth. Before long, Autu and Damut were covered with
it. They each tied colorful bandanas over their noses
to facilitate breathing. Soon the bandana was wet with
perspiration and caked with mud.

All of a sudden a wild-eyed longhorn advanced caus-
ing Autu's mount to rear up on its hind legs. Then,

the stirrup strap, Kelsey's unbraided variety, broke, throwing him to the ground. Damut quickly rolled behind a moss-encrusted boulder to escape the horns of the cow. The frightened horse took flight, galloping off at full speed. Damut approached the scene of the mishap and inquired, "Are you alright, Autu?"

"Yes, I am well– but not for long, I fear," a look of dread swept across his dust-laden face. "I will be beaten for this, it is for sure. Stone's horse is long gone."

Autu understood his friend's fear, as he, too had met with the wrath of Stone and Kelsey. Both beatings occurred for no discernible reason. But a lost horse would provide plenty of incentive for his friend to be beaten– or worse.

It was decided then and there that the beatings, starvation, torture, and enslavement of their people would end. They would have to kill Stone and Kelsey.

A plan was formulated in which all of the villagers were in agreement. Before they could find out about the missing horse, Stone and Kelsey's guns were confiscated, and water poured into their barrels, thereby disarming them. They were discreetly placed back in their original locations in the men's house.

Early the next morning a signal was given by one of the villagers to let the others know that Stone and Kelsey were in their kitchen having breakfast. All of a sudden a flurry of activity occurred, with the villagers rushing the men and knocking them to the ground. As the scuffle ensued Stone was hit in the head and killed with a rock.

Meanwhile, Kelsey had made his way from the kitchen to the sleeping house and took possession of his rifle. He aimed at the villagers and pulled the trigger. It wouldn't fire! The previous night's soaking of the gun barrel had done its job, preventing the awful man from killing anyone. The villagers, having discovered their cache of bows and arrows, hidden by Stone and Kelsey grabbed a weapon, took aim, and shot Kelsey dead. Both men were buried near the creek.

Chapter 12

The villagers, knowing there would be grave retaliation for the murder of Stone and Kelsey packed up what little they had and migrated to the northeast area of the lake. Here, at Badon-batin Island they thought they could hide and be safe.

They talked long into the night with the comfort of the stars as a familiar canopy. Djaska asked for another story. A cacophony of crickets trilled in the background.

"Look," said Mitabao, pointing his brown finger upward where a bat skimmed the night sky.

"Do you recall the story of Bat?" inquired Uncle.

"Bat was a maker of arrows," answered Mitabao.

"The best arrow maker," added Uncle. "Bat was given a piece of obsidian, and from that he produced a great many arrowheads."

"It's good that Bat did that," said Mitabao.

"Now is when we may really need the arrows and arrowheads," Uncle mused to himself, gazing south toward the Kelsey Ranch.

"Uncle, how did Coyote Create the Sun, Moon, and Stars?"

"Well," he said, "Coyote began by taking four exceptional pine boughs. After he painstakingly peeled the bark from them he attached special feathers of eagle and vulture with string made from milkweed fibers.

Next, he needed to pose himself in four distinct positions: on his head, then on his stomach, again on his back, and sitting straight up. After that, he scooped a ladle of water and flung it up into the sky. As the water began to make its way back to Earth it formed clouds all throughout the sky. This took four days.

Now Coyote cut an oak gall into the shape of a star with his obsidian knife and flung it up to the sky so that it became the sun.

Sun knew that the Moon was his mother and also that Coyote wanted a fire to be built so that he could have glowing coals. The hot coals could be thrown into the sky to make the stars. With that done, he created the animals and plants of the Earth and instructed them as to what their jobs were. It took eight days for the creation of everything to be completed. Having done all this he went to live in the mountains."

Their lives began to take on an old familiar pattern of mending nets, fishing, and other work, and after a few months they began to feel fairly safe and free once again.

That feeling of security was shattered one spring day. The United States Army had arrived at Kelsey's ranch and learned where the villagers were hiding.

A look-out of the People ran down the well-worn path. With fear in his eyes, and still panting he exclaimed, "The soldier just shot at me!"

There was much commotion as their worst fears played out before their eyes. A detachment of United States Army soldiers, under the direction of Captain Nathaniel Lyon were advancing on horseback. They stood tall on their mounts, wearing dark wool jackets encrusted with gleaming buttons. On either flank swung a sword and a rifle. Their black leather boots were encrusted with a thick film of dust from the ride up from Benicia.

The villagers scattered into the brush to hide, but to no avail. The soldier's weapons fired with deadly force. Many villagers took refuge in the waters of the lake, hiding among the thick reeds, and many submerged themselves. Some of the army soldiers were in boats and had the dual advantages of riding above the lake with their powerful weapons. The soldiers' intense weapons training was no match for the surprised villagers.

"Ready the cannon!" a soldier yelled. The once serene marsh exploded with unearthly clamor. A flock of woodducks sprang from the reeds, and hastily took flight. The blast of cannons could be heard for miles.

Some of the villagers bravely took up their slings and fired off innumerable shots from their powerful hunting weapons, while others fought back with bows and arrows. The army retaliated violently, however, killing over one hundred-fifty villagers in revenge for the deaths of Kelsey and Stone– two men who were well-known for torturing the villagers. The once clear and placid waters of the lake flowed red with the blood of the slaughtered men, women, and children.

Epilogue

A poppy-orange sun ascended the mist-covered lake while a flock of geese formed an arrow-shape as they withdrew, taking their winged leave. Beginnings and conclusions are timeless.

Colonel Redick McKee was sent to the People of the Water as an agent to bargain a treaty after the horrible massacre. But the white settlers were irate with this treaty and stormed Congress with a ceaseless crusade that, as a consequence obligated Congress to reject the treaty.

The brutality, bloodshed, and now rejection hurt the spirit of the People for a long, long while. It took much time for the bottomless wound to begin the healing process.

It was a time of new beginning; a time to rise up after arduous battle and construct life anew. They thought, "We can learn something from this terrible journey. We have to imagine a new home that we will build together by offering blessings and gratitude. We have our hope to bring us into the future, and the knowledge that in some way, we are all interconnected in nature- we, as people are all one, all related in spirit.

We must recognize this relation and allow it to take us forward in blessed health, and *not* allow this fear to root itself permanently and debilitate us forever. We must keep the good stories alive, and allow the good medicine of hope to take us into the future."

It was understood that the times were changing rapidly and that it was necessary for The People to move in a spirit of reconciliation. It was also understood that if anything was to be learned from this, that it would be necessary to build on the legacy of strong family and intimate ties with nature. Much work was needed to move toward living among many cultures. The prayer songs must not end.

The People understand the sacred gift that is the world. The understanding of the world involves an in-depth knowledge of the environment and all of its mysteries and magic. Claim the magic of each new sunrise and rejoice in the symbiotic cycle of life. There is a need more than ever to pay attention to the beauty of our surroundings. Respect those ideas and hold on to the gift. Keep dreaming so you won't forget.

The sacred Ghost Dances of the 1870s instigated by the Indian cultural leaders allowed the People to hold honor and respect once again; to reinstate a cohesive element again, in their swiftly changing lives. The goal was to dance with no hate, only good spirit. The essence of the dance was to convey the sacred.

Carry the Dream

Hear the voices from ancient times-
The songs of good spirit.
Those who danced here by the lake
Possessed the same dreams as ours-
To watch the hawk soar,
To pull fishing nets, full, from the water,
To pick blackberries and savor every
Aspect of their sun-burst qualities.
Listen, dance, and carry the dream.

Appendix I

From:

N. Lyon, Brevet Captain

Second Infantry, US Army

To:

Major E.R.S. Canby,

Monterey, California

Assistant Adjutant General

Headquarters Clear Lake Expd.

Anderson's Rancho, May 22 1850

In compliance with department orders (special) No. 24, I proceeded from Monterey to Benicia, where I arrived on the night of the 4th instant, and next morning took command of the expedition designed to proceed against the [Pomo] Indians on Clear Lake and Pit river, by virtue of Major Seawell's order of that date (a copy of which is herewith inclosed), and setting out next day (6th) from Benicia, I reached this position, at the south end of Clear Lake, on the 11th. The next day the dragoon company (lieut. Davidson) was detached round the western shores of the lake to cooperate with the infantry, to proceed by water up the lake. The Indians, on learning our approach, fled to an island at the northern extremity of the lake, opposite to which, and on the western shore of the lake, the command took position on the afternoon of the 14th, the Indians still gathering rapidly on the island. Lieut. Davidson, with Lieut. Haynes (mountain howitzer) attacked a rancho on the morning of this day, killing four and securing an Indian chief. Early on the morning of the 15th, the two shores being guarded, the landing on the island was effected, under a strong opposition from the Indians, who, perceiving us once upon their island, took flight directly, plunging into the water, among the heavy growth of tula which surrounds the islands, and which on the eastern and northern sides extends to the shores. Having rapidly cleared the island, I saw no alternative but to pursue them into the tula, and accordingly orders were given that the ammunition be slung around the necks of the men, and they proceed into the tula and pursue and destroy as far as possible. The tula was thus thoroughly searched, with severe protracted efforts, and with most gratifying results. The number killed I confidently report at not less than sixty, and doubt little that it is extended to a hundred and upwards. The Indians were supposed to be in number about 400. Their fire upon us was not effective, and no injury to the command occurred. The rancheria, extending about half way around the island, was burnt, together with a large amount of stores collected in it. Being satisfied that the Indian tribes on Russian river had participated in the murders of Stone and Kelsey and were not harboring one or two tribes known to be the most guilty, I now proceeded to the headwaters of that river, seeking first a tribe whose chief is called Chapo;

but finding the rancheria deserted t which my guide led me as his, I caused a thorough but ineffectual search to be make in the vicinity, and then proceeded down the river for about 22 miles to a tribe called the Yohaiyaks, among whom was Preesta and his tribe, the most active participants in the atrocious murders. I found them early on the morning of the 19th, on an island formed by a slough from Russian river, which was covered with dense undergrowth, and in the part where the Indians were mostly concealed were many trees, both dead and alive, in a horizontal position, interwoven with a heavy growth of vines. Their position being entirely surrounded, they were attacked under most embarrassing circumstances; but as they could not escape, the island soon became a perfect slaughter pen, as they continued to fight with great resolution and vigor till every jungle was routed. Their number killed I confidently report at not less than 75, and have little doubt it extended to nearly double that number. I estimate their whole number as somewhat greater than those on the island before mentioned. They were bold and confident, making known their position in shouts of encouragement to their men and defiance to us. Two of their shots took effect, wounding somewhat severely Corporal Kerry and private Patrick Coughlin, company 'G', the former in the shoulder and the latter in the thigh. A body of Indians supposed to have been concerned in the outrages at Kelsey's rancho, and who it was believed were harboring one of the tribes known to have been concerned in the Kelsey murder, lay about ten miles below; and in order that action might promptly be taken against them, according to the circumstances in which they might be found, I detached Lieutenant Davidson with his (dragoon) company to proceed hastily to the spot, so as to anticipate an alarm from the events just mentioned, and obtaining, with the assistance of Fernando Feliz, upon whose land these Indians lived, the facts, he was instructed to act accordingly. On arriving at Fernando Feliz's rancho he found the Indians had fled through fear. The intelligence that the hostile tribe was harbored by them proved unfounded, and no definite intelligence that they had participated in the murder aforesaid was ascertained.

I am, sir, very respectfully, your most obedient servant,

N. Lyon, Brevet Captain 2d Infantry,
Commanding Expedition.

Appendix II

COLLECTED DOCUMENTS ON THE CAUSES AND EVENTS
IN THE BLOODY ISLAND MASSACRE OF 1850.

1. CHIEF AUGUSTINE, ca. 1880.*/

Chief Augustine's Version of the Massacre.
--We will now give the story as related by
Augustine verbatim, taken down stenographically
at . the time of its recital. There were two
interpreters present, and the story was told
in a straightforward manner, and with but few
questions being asked. The people of Lakeport
have great confidence in his veracity as far as
he thinks that he is right. In the main his
story agrees with that already recited and which
was gleaned from the white settlers. Wherein it
does not we cannot, and presume no one else can
reconcile the two. Here is the narration:

"Salvador Vallejo had a claim on sixteen
leagues of land, around the west side of Clear

---

*/ L. L. Palmer. History of Napa and Lake
    Counties. California. Slocum, Bowen and Co.,
    San Francisco, 1881 (pp. 58-62).

Lake. Stone and Kelsey came and built an adobe
house at where Kelseyville now stands. They had
nothing but one horse apiece when they came into
the valley. They got all the Indians from Sanel,
Yokia, Potter Valley and the head of the lake
to come to the ranch, and of all those there he
chose twenty-six young Indians, all stout and
strong young men, and took them to the mines
on Feather River, and among them was Augustine.
This was in the summer time. In one month the
Indians had got for them a bag of gold as large
as a man's arm. They gave the Indians each a
pair of overalls, a hickory shirt and a red
handkerchief for their summer's work. They all
got home safely.

"They then made up another party of one
hundred young men, picked from the tribes as the
others had been, and went again to the mines.
This was late in the fall of the year or early
winter. They did not feed the Indians, and the
water was so bad that they could not drink it,
and they got sick, and two of them died there.
The Indians got dissatisfied and wanted to go
home. Finally, they told the Indians to go home.
On the road they all died from exposure and
starvation except three men, who eventually got
home. Two of these men are still living, and
their names are Miguel and Jim. Stone and Kelsey

got back before the three Indians did, but could give no satisfactory answer to the inquiries concerning the whereabouts of the Indians who had gone off with them. They were afraid of the Indians and did not go among them very much. At length the three arrived and told their story, but the Indians kept hoping that some more of them would come in the next spring, having spent the winter in the rancherias of some of the Sacramento Valley Indians, but in this they were doomed to disappointment.

"Stone and Kelsey took the gold they had got on their first trip and went to Sonoma Valley and bought one thousand head of cattle with it. It took six trips to get them all into Big Valley. There were twelve Indian vaqueros, of whom Augustine was the chief on each trip. They did not give these vaqueros very much to eat, and nothing for their wages. Stone and Kelsey also bought all the cattle that Vallejo had in the valley at this time. The whole valley was full of them, and they would number about two thousand head, any way, if not more.

"Stone and Kelsey used to tie up the Indians and whip them if they found them out hunting on the ranch anywhere and made a habit of abusing them generally. They got a lot of strong withes

which came from the mountain sides and were
very tough and kept them about the house for
the purpose of whipping the Indians with all
the time. When a friend of any of the vaqueros
came on a visit to the ranch, if they caught
them, they would whip them (the visitors) . The
Indians all the time worked well, and did not
complain. If the Indians questioned them about
the Indians who had died in the mountains, they
would whip them.

"Stone and Kelsey then tried to get the
Indians to go to the Sacramento River, near
Sutters Fort, and make there a big rancheria.
They would thus get rid of all except the young
men, used about the ranch as vaqueros, etc. The
Indians worked for two weeks, making ropes with
which to bind the young men and the refractory
ones, so as to be able to make the move Into
the Sacramento Valley. The old and feeble ones
they could drive, but they were afraid the young
men would fight them and kill them. They told
the Indians that, if they killed them, they
would come back again in four days, and the
Indians believed this, and thus they were held
in subjection. The Indian women made flour for
the ranch, with mortars, and it took them all
day to pound up a sufficient quantity for the use
of the place. The Indians were mad on account

of the fact that the others had died in the mountains, and then, when they wanted to move them off to the Sacramento Valley, they became still more enraged, and the plan was then set on foot to kill them.

"The Indians did all the work in building the adobe house, there being some four or five hundred of them engaged at it all the time for two months. They had to carry the water with which the adobes were mixed a distance of about five hundred yards, in their own grass buckets. Men and women all worked together. For all this number of people they only killed one beef a day, and they had no bread, nor anything else to eat except the meat. The more work the Indians did, the more they wanted them to do, and they got crosser and crosser with them every day.

"Augustine was sent to work for Ben. Kelsey in Sonoma Valley, and after about a month he came home to visit his friends, and as soon as Andy Kelsey saw him there he tied him up in a sweat-house on his feet and kept him standing there for a week. At the same time he tied up six others for the same period. When he had punished them he sent all but Augustine to Napa County, taking a lot of the other Indians with them, and just before starting off with them whipped

four of the number. They were sent down there
to build an adobe house for Salvador Vallejo,
and they were gone for a long time. He also took
Indians down to the lower valleys and sold them
like cattle or other stock.

"Finally the Indians made up their minds
to kill Stone and Kelsey, for, from day to day
they got worse and worse in their treatment of
them, and the Indians thought that they might as
well die one way as another, so they decided to
take the final and fatal step. The night before
the attack the Indians stole the guns of Stone
and Kelsey and hid them. Early in the morning
the Indians made the attack on them. Kelsey was
shot in the back with an arrow, which was shot
at him through a window. He then ran out of the
house, across the creek to where there was a
rancheria, and an old Indian caught him there
and struck him on the head with a stone and
killed him dead. Stone, when Kelsey was shot,
ran into a small house near the adobe and shut
the door. The Indians then cut the fastenings
of the door and he then tried to make his way
through the crowd to the big house, having in
his hand a large knife. He did not attack the
Indians with it, but used it as a protection for
himself. He had on a long-tailed coat, and as
he passed along the crowd was crushed in upon

him by the outer circles, and he was caught by the tail of the coat and jerked down and trampled upon, and his throat cut with his own knife, and left for dead. He jumped up and ran into the house, and the Indians supposed up stairs where the bows and arrows, which they had taken from the Indians, were stored. The Indians heard a rattling noise and thought he was up stairs, but he was not. It was only his death struggles which they heard. They feared to follow and see where he was, for if he had access to the bows and arrows he could use them as well as an Indian, and would thus probably kill some of them. The Indians buried both men, Kelsey near the rancheria where he fell, and Stone near the house. When the soldiers came up these bodies were taken up and they were both buried together.

"The Indians then all went to Scotts Valley and Upper Lake, or wherever else they pleased, as they all now felt that they had their liberty once more and were free men. The killing of Stone and Kelsey occurred in the winter. In the spring following the soldiers came to Kelsey's ranch and found that the Indians were on an island in a rancheria. They then sent and got their boats and cannon and went to Lower Lake, where they got some Indian guides to show them the way to the rancheria, at Upper Lake. When the soldiers came up they went over into Scotts Valley, and on the road found one Indian, whom they killed. The rest ran into the brush, and afterwards went to the rancheria at Upper Lake.' They killed two Indians in Scotts Valley. A part of the soldiers went from Lower Lake to Upper Lake in four boats, and the balance of them went on horseback around the Lake. They took the cannon by land, and passed through Scotts Valley on the road. They found a rancheria there and the Indians ran Into the brush. They fired the cannon twice into the brush, but did not kill any Indians.

"The two parties met at the point near Robinson's place, below Upper Lake. In Scotts Valley the Indians had a rifle, the one taken from Kelsey at the time of the killing. This they discharged at the soldiers which was the cause of their shooting the cannon at them. The entire party camped where the boats landed that night. In the morning early the party with the cannon went around the head of the lake and got on the north side of the island, and those in the boats went into the slough on the south side of the island. Before leaving, however, they killed their two Indian guides, one being shot and the other hung. They then began firing at the Indians with their small arms. Five Indians went out to give them battle; one with a sling and the other four with bows and arrows. <u>The cannon were not fired at all</u>. The Indians took to the tule and water and swam around and kept out of the way of the soldiers as much as possible, and there were only <u>sixteen</u> of them killed there that day. The soldiers then went over to Potter and Yokia Valleys. They did not find the Potter Valley Indians, but they had a fight with the Yokias. The Indians fought well considering their arras, and many of them were killed--over one hundred, at least. The soldiers returned to San Francisco by way of Sonoma. Afterwards about twenty men came up and sent word to the Indians in Scotts Valley to come to Kelsey's ranch and make a treaty. The Indians went down and the treaty was made. Ben. Moore drove the cattle of the Kelsey estate out of the valley. He had ten men with him."

Treaty of Peace. --Sometime during 1850 H. F. Teschmaker and a party came up to Lake County to make a treaty with the Indians. He sent out emissaries in all directions, and killed a lot of cattle and venison, and had a grand powwow. We do not know whether or not there are any papers on record in relation to this treaty; still, the Indians seemed to understand it, as will appear from Augustine's statement above, and were probably glad enough to adhere to its provisions. For this service and in payment for provisions said by Teschmaker to have been furnished by him to the Indians at this time, a bill was passed by the Legislature of the State allowing him several thousand dollars. The settlers generally, and all who know of the particulars of the affair assert that he was more than well paid for his time and trouble. ±/

±/ I know of no other record of H. Teschmaker's treaty with the Pomo. It may have been an unofficial act to reduce friction between whites and Indians. In 1851 Col. R. McKee entered into a treaty with the Pomo, but the U.S. Senate refused to ratify this agreement. On the 1851 treaty see The Eighteen Unratified Treaties of 1851-1852 Between The California Indians and The United States Government. Archaeological Research Facility, 1972 (pp. 81-88).

Bibliography

Allen, Elsie
1972 *Pomo Basket Making,* Naturegraph Publishers,
Happy Camp, CA.

Bancroft, Hubert Howe
1886 History of California Vols. I-V11,The History
Company Publishers, San Francisco.

Barrett, S.A.
1933 *Pomo Myths,* Cannon Printing Co., Milwaukee, WI.

Brown, Vinson and Douglas Andrews
1990 The Pomo Indians of California and Their
Neighbors, Naturegraph Publishers, Happy Camp, CA.

"Collected Documents on the Causes and Events
in the Bloody Island
Massacre of 1850", 1973, Heizer, Anthropological
Research Facility, U.C. Berkeley.

Comstock, Esther S.
1979 *Vallejo and the Four Flags,* Comstock
Bonanza Press.

Davis, James T.
1961 *Trade Routes and Economic Exchange Among
the Indians of California,* University of California
Archaeological Survey, Berkeley, CA.

Gifford, Edward W. and Gwendoline Harris Block
  1990 *California Indian Nights,* University of Nebraska
  Press, Lincoln and London.

Gifford, Edward Winslow
  1926 *Clear Lake Pomo Society,* University of California
  Press, Berkeley, CA.

Goodrich, Jennie and Claudia Lawson, Vana Parrish
Lawson
  1980 *Kashaya Pomo Plants,* Heyday Books, Berkeley, CA.

Grbasic, Z. and V. Vuksic
  1989 *The History of Calvary,* Facts on File, New York

Heizer, Robert F.
  Assembled and Edited:
  Collected Documents on the Causes and Events in
  the Bloody Island Massacre of 1850

Heizer, Robert F.
  1974 *The Destruction of California Indians*, University
  of Nebraska Press, Lincoln and London.

Heizer, R.F. and M.A. Whipple
  1971 *The California Indians– A Source Book,* University
  of CA Press, Berkeley.

Heizer, Robert F. & Alan F Almquist
  1971 *The Other Californians– Prejudice and
  Discrimination under Spain, Mexico, and the United
  States to 1920,* University of California Press,
  Berkeley, CA.

Hurtado, Albert L.
1988 *Indian Survival on the California Frontier,*
Yale University Press, New Haven and London.

Kroeber, A.L.
1925 *Handbook of the Indians of California,*
Dover Pub., Inc. New York.

Loeb, Edwin M.
1926 *Pomo Folkways* University of California Press,
Berkeley, CA.

Margolin, Malcom, Editor
1993 *The Way We Lived* Heyday Books, Berkeley, CA.

Menefee, C.A.
1873 *Historical and Descriptive Sketchbook of Napa,
Sonoma, Lake, and Mendocino,*
James D. Stevenson, Ph.D., Fairfield, CA.

Merriam, C. Hart Collected and Edited
1993 *The Dawn of the World,* University of Nebraska
Press, Lincoln, Nebraska.

Moratto, Michael J.
1984 *California Archaeology,* Harcourt Brace,
New York, NY.

National Archives
"Treaty Made and Concluded at Camp Lu-Pi-Yu-Ma",
and Letter from N.Lyon, Brevet Captain, To Major
E.R.S. Canby, May 22, 1850.

"News From Native California", Vol. 13, No. 4
Summer 2000, Heather Hafleigh, Indian Vaqueros
of California.

Parker, Dr. John
Of Archaeological Research, Lucerne, CA
https://www.academia.edu/5539505/The_Kelsey_
Brothers_A_California_Disaster

Rosenus, Alan
1995 *General M.G. Vallejo and the Advent of
the Americans,* University of New Mexico Press,
Albuquerque.

Sarris, Dr. Greg
1993 *Keeping Slug Woman Alive– A Holistic Approach to
American Indian Texts,* University of California Press,
Berkeley, CA.

Sarris, Dr. Greg
1994 *Mabel McKay– Weaving the Dream,* University of
California Press, Berkeley, CA.

Scavone, Kathleen
1999 *Anderson Marsh State Historic Park– A Walking
History, Prehistory, Flora, and Fauna Tour of a California
State Park,* Bradford Creek Publishers.

Slocum, Bowen, and Bowen Publishers
1881 *History of Napa and Lake Counties, California,*
San Francisco, CA.

Smithsonian Institution
1978 *Handbook of North American Indians* Vol. 8.

Trafzer, Clifford E.
1989 *California's Indians and the Gold Rush,*
Sierra Oaks Publishing Co., Newcastle, CA.

About the Author

Kathleen Scavone, M.A., educator for 24 years, is a freelance writer, potter and photographer. She is the author of *Anderson Marsh State Historic Park– A Walking History, Prehistory, Flora, and Fauna Tour of a California State Park*. She has also written *Native Americans of Lake County, California* and *Lake County Poetry*. Her work can be seen in the *Santa Rosa Press Democrat, Lake County News*, the *Napa Valley Register, News From Native California*, the *Education Center*, etc. She freelances articles for numerous publications, and writes essays and plays. She regularly wrote *NASA* space articles as one of *NASA* and *JPL*'s Solar System Ambassadors for over a dozen years.

Made in the USA
Middletown, DE
01 May 2024

53726040R00064

"This story is a *must read* for anyone wanting to understand Native California lifeways just before the European invasion and the disruption that followed."

—Dr. John Parker
Archaeologist, Archaeological Research, Lucerne, CA
wolfcreekarcheology.com

The "*People of the Water*" is a story of one culture's love of life and the world around them. Kathleen Scavone paints a picture that time-travels the reader back to a Clear Lake Pomo village in the mid 1800's where actual Native American cultural traditions, technologies, beliefs, and knowledge are portrayed, as they would have been learned and experienced then. The arrival of Europeans and their disrupting interaction with the Indigenous People is explored as seen from the perspective of the Native Culture.

Though some of the actual events and experiences in the story are fictionalized, all of the proceedings outlined in the story are based on actual knowledge of Clear Lake Pomo culture as provided by tribal elders that were interviewed by ethnographers in the late 1800's and early 1900's.

Kathleen Scavone, M.A., is an educator, freelance writer, potter and photographer. She has written the book *Anderson Marsh State Historic Park- A Walking History, Prehistory, Flora, and Fauna Tour of a California State Park; Native Americans of Lake County, California* and *Lake County Poetry*. She freelances articles for numerous publications like the *Press Democrat, Lake County News*, the *Napa Valley Register, News From Native California*, and the *Education Center, Inc.* in North Carolina. She also regularly wrote *NASA* space articles as a *JPL* Solar System Ambassador.

Visit Kathleen at her website at: *KathleenScavone.com*

Bradford Creek Publishing Company

Cover Photo by Kathleen Scavone
Copyright © 2021-2014 by Kathleen Scavone

Cover designed and interior reformatting
by Leo Baquero, leo_baquero@hotmail.com
layoutadaptationdesign.com